Steven Herrick was born in Brisbane, the youngest of seven children. At school his favourite subject was soccer, and he dreamed of football glory while he worked at various jobs. For the past twenty-five years he's been a full-time writer and regularly performs his work in schools throughout the world. Steven lives in the Blue Mountains with his partner Cathie, a belly dance teacher. They have two adult sons, Jack and Joe.

www.stevenherrick.com.au

Also by Steven Herrick

POOKIE ALEERA IS NOT MY BOYFRIEND

STEVEN HERRICK

UQP

First published 2012 by University of Queensland Press
PO Box 6042, St Lucia, Queensland 4067 Australia

www.uqp.com.au
uqp@uqp.uq.edu.au

Typeset in 12.5/18 pt Adobe Garamond by Post Pre-press Group, Brisbane
Printed in Australia by McPherson's Printing Group

Cataloguing-in-Publication Data
National Library of Australia

Herrick, Steven, 1958-
Pookie Aleera is not my boyfriend / Steven Herrick.
For primary school age.

A823.3

ISBN (pbk) 978 0 7022 4928 0
ISBN (pdf) 978 0 7022 4850 4
ISBN (epub) 978 0 7022 4851 1
ISBN (kindle) 978 0 7022 4852 8

University of Queensland Press uses papers that are natural, renewable
and recyclable products made from wood grown in sustainable
forests. The logging and manufacturing processes conform to
the environmental regulations of the country of origin.

The publisher recommends all recipes in this book be made under
adult supervision.

In the past twenty-five years, I've visited over three thousand schools to read my work and talk to the students and teachers. So, finally, I'd like to dedicate a book to all the people who've welcomed me into their school lives.

To the students: may all your days be sunny.

To the teachers: may all your students be smiling.

To the librarians: may all your books be borrowed.

RACHEL

My town
is exactly
four hundred and twenty-two kilometres
from the ocean.
I check the distance
driving home from holidays
with Mum and Dad
the day before school begins
and while Bondi Beach
gets frothy waves
of cool, salty water on white sand
my town suffers
waves of dust storms
and locust plagues
and heat that melts the bitumen
and the first thing I do
when we get home
after driving all day
is run down to the dam
in the near paddock
and dive in.
The water is warm and brown.

My toes squelch in the mud
while the windmill clanks.
A pond-skater buzzes the surface
and starlings fantail
across the sky
the day before school begins.

LAURA

My new teacher
wears a flowing summer dress
with red pianos printed
on white linen.
Her hair is crow-black and messy
and she pulls it back
from her face
and ties it with a red ribbon.
She wears black ballet shoes
and casually sits on her desk
before asking us
to tell her something, one thing,
that we like about ourselves.
Selina, Mick, Cameron, Pete and Rachel
immediately
raise their hands
while I slink as low as possible
behind my desk.

SELINA

Ms Arthur said we should
bring in a photo of ourselves,
our favourite,
to paste on the Class 6A wall
and we could draw a design
around the photo
with our name, in bright colours.
And underneath our photo
we could write,
once a week,
what we've done lately
or what made us happy, or sad.
'Just like Facebook,' I said.

On Tuesday we spent all morning
drawing our names in big letters
with swirling colours
of red, yellow, green and blue.
Except Cameron
who wrote his name in *tiny letters*.
His writing was so small
you had to go really close

just to see if it was there at all.
And he'd chosen a thumbnail photo
of when he was a baby
lying in a cot asleep.
Cameron spent the whole morning
admiring his *little* photo and his *teeny* name
surrounded by glaring white cardboard.
Sometimes he stepped back
and looked at the photo from different angles,
like an artist.
Then he'd move close and adjust it,
just slightly.
Finally Ms Arthur couldn't stand it any longer.
She asked Cameron
if he planned to add anything
to his cardboard.
Cameron looked shocked
and said, in his usual loud voice,
'No way, Ms.
I want to have lots of space
to write about everything I think!'

MICK

I'm staring out the window
minding no one's business but my own
because Ms Arthur is teaching maths
and that's not really my go.
What do we have calculators for?
Charlie Deakin from 5C comes in with a note
and Ms Arthur tells me the Principal
'requires my presence in his office'.
So I follow Charlie along the verandah
and he's smirking the whole time
because no one gets called out of class
for good news,
it's always trouble,
but I don't say anything
and I don't act nervous
because I haven't done anything wrong,
not lately anyway.
Well, not that Mr Hume knows
and I trust my classmates not to tell anyway.
Charlie Deakin is still grinning
like he's won a prize,
yeah, first-prize boofhead.

He knocks on the Principal's door
and says to me,
'Hume's madder than a nest of bull ants.'
Charlie Deakin opens the door
and walks away down the hallway
leaving me standing there
with Mr Hume looking at me
and he's not smiling.

ALEX

I thought it was a simple question, really.
Ms Arthur asked each of us to stand up, in turn,
and say what we want to be
when we grow up.
The first five students said,
'Farmer.'
Then Rachel said,
'Pilot.'
And we went slowly around the class,
'Teacher.'
'Doctor.'
'Truck driver.'
'Vet.'
'Soldier.'
When it was my turn,
I stood up
and, in a very clear voice, said,
'A dad.'
A few people giggled
as if I'd said something rude,
or stupid.
I sat down again,

red-faced and confused.
It was the truth.
I wanted to be a dad.
I've never seen my dad
and I wouldn't wish that
on anyone.
Rachel stood up, again,
and said,
'Ms Arthur, I want to be a pilot
and a mum!'

MICK

'Yeah, he's my brother
and I'm supposed to look after him
but it was lunchtime, Mr Hume,
and the canteen has a special –
two dollars for a hot dog and drink.
You should try it, sir.
Mrs Casey says it's a low-fat dog,
if you're worried.
Not that you need to be worried, sir.
Not at all.

Back to my brother,
well, he's been talking all week
about wanting to fly, sir.
I thought he meant in a plane.
You know, like normal people.

You've got to admit it was pretty impressive
climbing on the roof of the groundsman's shed.
Maybe planting wattles that close
wasn't such a good idea
even if they bloom yellow all summer.

I don't think he meant to jump, sir.
He was probably just checking the wind speed.

No, sir. I did not give him
the feathers, the sticks or the glue.
He'll be in big trouble with Mum
when she discovers the spare doona is empty.

Yes, it's true, last year
I told all the boys in Kindy
they had to wear a dress in honour
of Darcy Dress, the famous inventor.
I got a week's detention,
and Mum had me sewing,
can you believe it,
sewing dresses, as punishment!
I've learnt my lesson, sir.
So, honestly, truly and no kidding,
I didn't tell Jacob to jump off the roof.

How is Mr Korsky, sir?
It must have been a shock,
having an eight-year-old land on your back.
But I hear it broke Jacob's fall, sir.
Mr Korsky is a hero!

Maybe we should celebrate,
have a special lunch?
Ask Mrs Casey to order in pizzas?
Sorry, sir, I know that's off the point,
so, trust me,
I will talk to Jacob about
outlandish flying experiments
and jumping off the roof,
I promise.'

JACOB

I didn't see him.
I was looking up,
flapping my arms
as fast as they could go.
I only looked down
when my wings fell off.
That wasn't supposed to happen.
Mr Korsky was leaning over,
filling the watering can.
What could I do?
I wrapped my arms tightly around his neck
to break my fall
and we both hit the ground,
like two hay bales
that rolled off the back of Dad's truck.

Mr Korsky said a few words
I'm pretty sure are illegal at school,
words my dad said once
when he was fixing the chook shed
and the hammer slipped.
I reckon it's okay Mr Korsky swore

because I still had my arms tight around his neck
and maybe he thought I was a criminal
trying to steal his wallet,
his gardening tools
or his bright blue watering can.
All those swear words
would have scared away any thief.
I was ready to run, too,
only it hurt in my arms, legs, back, ribs
and other parts I can't name.
It felt better not moving,
lying on my back and crying seemed the best idea.
So that's what I did.
Mr Korsky looked like he wanted to join me.

PETE

Nan says the road to our house
is like a train track without the rails.
Just stones and ruts and potholes.
It goes on for ages
and last year the shire council
decided the school bus couldn't take it anymore.
Nah, they didn't fix the road,
they stopped the service.
It's only our family who lives out here.
Now we walk up Peaks Hill
and cut through the Jensen farm,
stepping over millions of cowpats
and dodging the stinging nettle
to reach the other road
where the bus *does* stop.
It takes me and Ursula twenty minutes
because she's only six years old
and I have to hold her hand,
even if she doesn't want me to.

We only have to do it for another few weeks
because the council has decided
to bitumen our road.
True.
All because the ambulance didn't make it on time
when Grandpa had a heart attack last month.
If it was a proper road . . .
but it wasn't and even though Dad and me
lifted him into the Land Rover
and Dad drove
like I've never seen him drive before,
we only made it halfway to town.
The ambulance put Grandpa on the metal trolley
that clanked and creaked
and we jumped in the back.
But it didn't do any good.

I held Ursula's hand at the funeral too.
It was warm and soft and small.
I looked at her hand in mine for ages,
instead of looking at Grandpa's coffin.

CAMERON

Last night
Mum had her flamenco classes,
Dad was working late
and my sister Simone was at netball
so
I was alone
and I'd told everyone
I was cooking my own dinner
and I promised to clean up afterwards,
no worries.
I looked in the freezer –
frozen pizza,
chicken wings
and yesterday's leftover stew.
I checked the fridge –
eggs,
bacon
and the last slice of Simone's cheesecake.
I searched the cupboard –
cans of minestrone soup,
baked beans
and an unopened packet of Tim Tams,

Mum's favourite.
I stood in the kitchen for hours
trying to decide.
I was so hungry that I wanted everything . . .
but where to start?

To give myself time to choose
I sat in front of the television
with the remote,
flicking from channel to channel –
Discovery had a virtual trip to the moon
and there were cartoons on both Disney channels
and soccer,
cricket
and rugby league
on the sports channels
and there was a *Simpsons* hour
starting in five minutes
and I didn't think that was enough time
to cook anything
so I switched off the television
and turned on the computer
and surfed the net
to see if I could find the games site
I was on yesterday

and I got caught up in a chat with my mate Alex
but he couldn't talk for long
'cause his mum had just called him for dinner
which reminded me
I still hadn't eaten
so I went to the kitchen
and placed two slices of bread on a plate,
then held the honey jar high above the bread
and squeezed,
great dollops of liquid gold dribbled over the bread
(and the plate and the bench . . . and the floor).
I promised myself I'd clean it up
before anyone got home.
But first, the sweet dinner!
I sat on the bench
and lowered the soggy bread into my mouth,
chewing and smacking my lips, eyes closed.
A honey empire and I was King!

After eating
I went to the lounge,
put my feet up
and stuffed lots of pillows all around me
before switching on *The Simpsons*.

That's all I remember.
This morning I woke up in my own bed
so Dad must have carried me in
and I missed *The Simpsons*
and I didn't cook anything
and I didn't play any computer games
but, most importantly,
I didn't open Mum's Tim Tams
and eat them all!

JACOB

At the hospital
the kind nurse bandaged my right arm
all the way up to my elbow
and down to my fingers.
She also put some smelly yellow liquid
on my scratched knee.
As she did, she smiled and said it might hurt.
I said, 'Not as much as falling off a shed.'
The doctor shone a torch in my eyes
and put a very cold hearing-aid-thing to my chest,
telling me to breathe normally.
I said that was the only way
I knew how to breathe.
The nurse said she was going to check my pulse
and my blood pressure
before letting Mum take me home.
As we were leaving, she said,
'Don't go jumping off any more sheds.'
I waved and answered,
'No way. Next time I'll jump out of a tree.'

Mum and the nurse stood
with their mouths hanging open,
until I smiled and said,
'Only joking.'

SELINA

Every morning this week it's been the same.
Ms Arthur calls out the roll.
Alphabetically.
Starting with Pete Ancich,
followed by Tiffany Brown,
then me, Selina Chandler.
Everyone says, 'Here, Ms'
or, 'Present, Ms.'
But we're all waiting
for Ms Arthur to call out Cameron's name.
Because,
without fail,
Cameron jumps out of his chair,
salutes Ms Arthur
and says, in his loudest voice,
'Present and ready for action, Ms!'
The first time he did it,
Ms Arthur frowned and muttered,
'Thank you.'
We could see she was a little bothered.
But after a week of Cameron
saluting and shouting,

she realised he wasn't going to stop
and he wasn't hurting anybody,
except maybe our eardrums!
So now, once in a while,
instead of just calling out, 'Cameron Knowles',
Ms Arthur stands to attention and says,
'Sergeant Knowles!'
Cameron smiles and almost leaps from his chair.
Everyone giggles,
except Cameron.
He's too busy yelling!

MR KORSKY

When all the children
have gone home
I circle the schoolyard
picking up lunch wrappers
and chip packets
and discarded hats –
the Lost Property basket is overflowing –
and soft-drink cans
and lolly wrappers
and every day
someone leaves a half-eaten apple
wedged
in the branch of the sunshine wattle
as if they're leaving me a gift.
I shake my head
and fling it in the rubbish,
wondering why they couldn't
practise their throwing
and aim for the bin near the toilet block
instead of making me stretch into the tree
when I'm two years off retiring
and the only hair on my head

grows out of my ears and my nose
and
hello . . .
what's this . . .
the half-eaten apple
resting in the same place . . .
except underneath is a note
and printed in very neat handwriting
are the words,
'Please, sir.
The apple isn't rubbish . . .
it's for the birds.'
I stand there holding the paper
and as if on cue
I hear a chirp from above.
A rosella sits high in the tree
watching me.
I put the apple back,
the note I tuck in my pocket.
One less thing to pick up.

ALEX

My brother
goes into his bedroom
puts on his favourite
grunge rock DVD,
turns it up really loud,
jumps on his bed
singing louder than the music
and
starts air guitar!
He waves his right arm
up and down
like a crazy windmill
banging the strings
his fingers twitch and move
faster than the speed of light
as his face contorts
in weird air guitar poses.
Then he jumps off his bed
and lands on his knees,
sliding along the shiny timber floor
still playing
furious air guitar.

Mum just smiles
and keeps reading her book.
I'm trying to do homework
so I ask Mum
if he could turn it down,
and what does she say?
'In a minute. Let him have his fun.'

My brother is twenty-six years old.

LAURA

Mum says they named me
after their favourite song,
'with a chorus of strings and soaring vocals',
that's how Mum describes it.
And that song, which they'd sing over and over, is
'Tell Laura, I Love Her'.
Mum says she'd always cry whenever she heard it,
when Dad and her were . . .
you know, boyfriend and girlfriend . . .
in love . . .
before they got married.
Mum says when they came home from the doctor
after learning she was pregnant,
they agreed to call the child *Laura*
even if it was a boy!
Mum says,
she knew I'd be a girl
because of the name.
She calls it destiny.

Dad left home two years ago
and now whenever he phones from the city,

and I'm not home
he says to Mum,
'Tell Laura, I love her.'
Only I don't think he sings it into the phone.

RACHEL

This morning
Ms Arthur writes
NIGHT SKY
on the whiteboard
and asks us to try to describe it
in one sentence.
Everyone looks around the room
nervously
waiting for someone to raise their hand.
Ms Arthur leans patiently on her desk
until I can't stand the silence any longer.
I raise my hand and say,
'It's like a blanket for the earth to sleep under.'
Ms Arthur smiles.
Cameron raises his hand and says,
'It's deeper than the Grand Canyon!'
Mick adds,
'And wider than the Pacific Ocean.'
Selina says, 'It's where shooting stars
write their name.'
My favourite is when Alex says,
'It's lightning graffiti!'

And suddenly everyone is raising their hands
and calling out,
'An ink ocean!'
'Thick chocolate sauce with sprinkles for stars . . .'
'. . . and the moon is the cook's fingernail!'

After Ms Arthur
has erased the words
NIGHT SKY
from the whiteboard
and we're knuckling down to maths
Cameron raises his hand
and asks,
'Ms, can you write two words
on the board every morning
and we'll try to describe it?'
Instead of answering,
Ms Arthur walks to the whiteboard and writes,
YES, CAMERON.

CONSTABLE DAWE

'Good morning, Class 6A.
My name is Constable Dawe
and I'm here . . .
what's that, young man?
No, my name is not *Constable*,
it's Brian,
Constable is my title,
my rank in the police force.
Yes, young lady,
like a General,
only we don't have generals,
just commissioners
and sergeants
and constables
of which I'm one.
And I'm here to talk about road safety.
Can anyone tell me something about road safety?
Well, yes, you're right,
it should be called pedestrian safety
because no one can hurt a road,
it's just a large piece of concrete.

True, young man,
if someone dropped a bomb on the road
that would destroy it
but I don't know anyone with a bomb, do you?
Yes, terrorists have bombs
but we don't have terrorists in town
not last time I looked anyway,
back to road safety, *pedestrian* safety, if you will.
Can anyone tell me what we should do
before crossing the road?
Pardon?
Wear clean underwear!
Who told you that?
Your mother . . .
in case you're in an accident.
Well, I'm here to prevent you having an accident
so
apart from wearing clean underwear,
what else should we do
before crossing the road?
Yes,
before crossing the road
we should first leave the house,
but, Class 6A,

let's imagine, shall we,
that we're all on the footpath
in clean underwear
and about to cross the road.
What should we do to avoid accidents?
No, wearing a life jacket won't save us
not unless the road is flooded
and it hasn't been flooded since 1978, I believe,
so take off the life jackets
and
and
and
yes, young lady, that's correct
look both ways
no
not up and down
not forward and behind
look left and right
and then
and then
no, don't run like heck, young man,
look left again
then quickly walk to the other side.
Well done, Class 6A.

Now, can you tell me
what we should do on bicycles?
Not fall off . . . yes.
Not do wheelies when your dad's watching . . . yes.
But what should we be wearing?
Thank you, young man,
we know about clean underwear
we've heard enough about clean underwear
what else should we be wearing . . .
on our heads . . .
no, I was not saying we should wear
clean underwear on our heads!
No, not a sunhat,
something harder than a sunhat, perhaps,
a helmet
yes,
a helmet.

I think we'll leave it there for today, Class 6A.
Next time
we'll talk about water safety . . .
yes, okay, *swimmer safety*, if you must.
Without the underwear hopefully.
Stop laughing, Class 6A,

I wasn't suggesting nude swimming.
We will not be nude swimming next week
or any other week
we'll be . . .

Thank you once again, Class 6A.'

SELINA

Mr Korsky brought his nephew Nigel to school
to help him because poor Mr Korsky
has to wear a neck brace for another week,
you know,
after the unfortunate flying Jacob incident.
Nigel has a nose ring,
two earrings
and an eyebrow ring.
He also has a tattoo of a snake
slithering up his arm
and when he flexes his bicep
it looks like the serpent is about to strike.
He showed all of Year Six this trick at lunchtime
when he was emptying the rubbish bins.
Nigel says he used to come to this school
ten years ago
and he tried to jump off the shed as well
only he wasn't flying;
he was ambushing
his worst enemy, Mark Banbridge.
He told us about Mark
and some girl called Robyn

and how Mark
shouldn't have got so friendly with her.
I swear when he was talking
the tattoo on his arm grew bigger and meaner,
and I moved to the outside of the circle,
just in case.
Cameron asked Nigel
if getting all those piercings hurt
and Nigel said,
'Nah, the only thing that hurt was my eardrums.'
'Eardrums?' I asked.
'Yeah. You should have heard the noise
Dad made when he saw all my rings!'

CAMERON

My dad makes things up.
I know that now,
but when I was young
and my ears were even younger,
I believed everything he said.
Like the day we sat in the park
and watched the teenagers
throwing a bright green plastic ring,
a radical Frisbee,
and I asked Dad what it was called.
He said, quick as you please,
'A parisian ring'
and I practised saying the words
over and over
sitting beside Dad
watching the teenagers catch and dive and fling
and I saved all my pocket money for three months,
safely hidden in a jar,
the lid closed tight, under my bed
until I had enough money to buy one.
I walked into every shop in town asking,

'Do you sell a parisian ring?'

They searched their computer lists,
they asked the boss,
they scratched their heads,
no one sold a parisian ring,
no one had even heard of it.

So at dinner I asked Dad
the next time he went to the city
could he buy one
and I handed him the money,
all my savings.
Mum and Dad stared at the coins
piled between the mashed potato
and the gravy jug.
Dad said,
'Parisian ring?'
He looked at Mum
and Simone
and then back at me.
I made the throwing motion with my hand
and repeated the name
over and over.

How could he forget?
'You know, in the park,
the green plastic thing.'
And then he remembered.

A week later
I got home from school
and there was a parcel
neatly wrapped on the table
and a card with my name on it.
I unwrapped the parcel
as quick as my hands could move.
It was green
and in splashy black writing on the top
were the words,
Astro Frisbee.
What!
Astro who?
Then I turned it over
and scrawled in black texta,
in writing just like Dad's,
were the words,
parisian ring.

I looked up and saw Dad smiling
and he said,
'It's a good name, don't ya reckon?'
We went outside into the backyard
and played until dark,
me and Dad
and the parisian ring.

JACOB

My brother Mick broke his arm
when he was nine years old.
I only sprained mine.
The day he came home from hospital
he let me draw a dragon on the plaster cast.
I was five years old
so it wasn't a very good drawing
just lots of colours
with big round circles and horns,
and fire coming out of his mouth.
Mick showed it to everyone in school
and he got me to sign my name on it
and said I'd be a famous artist one day
'like Michelangelo'
who I thought was a Mutant Ninja Turtle.
Everyone at school wanted to sign their name
but Mick wouldn't let them.
He said it wasn't a cast anymore,
it was *Jacob's art gallery*.
Every night I coloured in the dragon
on Mick's arm
and the next day he'd show everyone at recess.

I look at the bandage on my arm now.
The doctor says I was lucky I didn't break it.
What do doctors know?

SELINA

Ms Arthur walked into class
and said, 'Good morning, 6A'
and we all said,
'Good morning, Ms.'
Except Cameron, who yelled,
'GOOD MORNING, MS!'
Ms Arthur smiled patiently
and asked, 'How are you today, Cameron?'
'GOOD, MS,' he shouted.
Ms Arthur sighed, gently,
and said, 'Remember, class, I explained
you should say *well* not *good*.
I'm asking about your health,
not your moral standing.'
She walked to her desk
and sat down.
'Now, Cameron, how are you today?'
'WELL, MS!'
'And you, Rachel?'
'Well, thanks, Ms.'
'Mick?'
'Very well, Ms.'

'And you, Alex?'
'Sick as a drunk parrot, Ms.'
Then he ran out of the room,
all the way to the toilet
and didn't return until after recess.

RACHEL

At recess I go to the canteen
and buy a can of lemonade
and I ask Mrs Casey
if I can have an extra plastic cup.
I pour two equal cups of lemonade
and I sit on the verandah
watching the fizz fizzle out,
for what seems like hours.
When the lemonade is finally . . . fizzless,
I take both cups into the sick bay
where Alex is sitting on the daybed
looking very sad and lonely
until
I offer him a cup,
'My mum says it helps.'
Alex tries to smile,
all the time holding his stomach.
I stand in the doorway
and
he sits on the daybed
both of us
drinking

the flat lemonade
until there's none left
and I say,
'I can get some more if you want?'
But the bell rings
which is lucky
because I don't think I have enough money
for another can.

SELINA

As soon as we finish roll call
Cameron raises his hand,
'Ms, I've lost my mobile phone.'
Ms Arthur says,
'Have you tried phoning it, Cameron,
to see if anyone answers?'
And Cameron replies,
'I can't, Ms. I don't have a phone
to phone my phone because I've lost my phone.'

PETE

Ms Arthur says
that when she lived in the city
sometimes
in the middle of the night
she'd hear a fire-engine siren
and she'd imagine
an old man
stuck in an apartment building
with the kitchen on fire
and the man would be coughing and spluttering
with smoke billowing from the open window
and the neighbours,
all in their nighties and pyjamas
would be frantically spraying water
from their garden hoses
even though it would never be enough
and the dogs would start howling
as they heard the siren getting nearer
and the fire truck would screech to a halt outside
and all the men
would grab ropes and ladders
and hoses and extinguishers

and axes to break down the door
and . . .

Everyone in class
is waiting for the end of the story . . .

Ms Arthur shivers a little,
even though it's blazing hot outside,
and she tells us
she'd stay awake all night
thinking exactly what we're thinking now.
Did the old man survive?
Did the firemen make it on time?

CAMERON

Banned!
For life!
That's what Mrs Davenport said
when she caught me
reading the comic
at the back of her shop on Friday
and I only had two pages left to finish.
I still don't know
if Spiderman survived
or if the Green Goblin's
superhero insecticide was fatal!
All week
I'd been careful to read only ten pages
each afternoon
hidden behind the shelves
until the suspense sucked me in
and I forgot where I was
and that's when
Mrs Davenport (the Grey Goblin!)
swooped
grabbing the comic
except

I held on tight
and the paper ripped.
I don't know who was the most surprised
but
Mrs Davenport
said a few words
popular with truck drivers and drunks
before pointing to the door
and sentencing me to
life imprisonment,
no,
life *ex*prisonment.
And where will I go when Dad
flicks a dollar my way
and asks me to buy him a newspaper?

LAURA

Mum has never said
that I can't look at her treasures,
not in so many words.
So before she gets home from work,
after I've put the chicken and potatoes
in the oven for dinner,
I go into her sewing room
to the bottom drawer of her cupboard.
I take out the photo album
and slowly turn each page.
I never get bored,
no matter how many times
I see the same photos
of Mum and Dad at university.
Dad's haircut makes me giggle,
his ears stick out like a bat!
Mum looks so young,
wearing jeans and riding boots
and a T-shirt with an anti-war slogan.
Mum never wears T-shirts!
In one photo they're standing
in front of Dad's car

and he's got his arm around her shoulder
and she's hugging him
and her face is turned away from the camera.
It's like they're sharing a secret
and no one else can ever know what it is.
When Mum and me have dinner at night,
and Mum's dabbing butter on my potatoes
and I'm pouring the cold water into our glasses,
I so much want her to tell me the secret.
The secret to how she was ever so happy.

SELINA

As soon as we finish roll call this morning
Cameron raises his hand,
'Ms, I've lost my mobile phone again.'
Ms Arthur says,
'Have you tried calling it, Cameron?'
and Cameron replies,
'I can't, Ms, it doesn't have a name.'

JACOB

At lunchtime
on my first day at school
without the bandage
I visit Mr Korsky in his work shed.
He points at my arm and says,
'How's the damage, laddie?'
I hold it up
all white and skinny
and stiff and still a little sore
and I say,
'Free! Free at last!'
Mr Korsky laughs
then he rubs his back
and looks a little worried
as if I might jump on him again
so I say,
'No more flying, sir.'
He smiles,
'Not without a plane, laddie.'

MICK

I've never seen so many kids in a circle before,
all pushing and trying to get a look at
whatever is inside the ring.
I'd like to know just what that is
but I'm stuck on detention
for what I did to Pete's watermelon.
How could I know it would make such a mess
if I dropped it from the verandah?
That's why Pete brought it to school
only he didn't want to throw it
on account of School Rules.
I told him I'd never seen a rule that read,
No dropping watermelons from verandahs.

I stretch my legs under the table
and look at the clock on the wall,
counting down the seconds,
fifteen, fourteen, thirteen . . .
right on time,
Ms Arthur comes into the room
and tells me to 'not use fruit as a projectile again'.
That's an easy one to promise,

especially when I've got all my fingers crossed.
Teachers never check those things.
You'd think they'd learn that stuff
at university, wouldn't you?
Anyway, I run down the stairs two at a time
and nearly knock Laura Wright over.
She's eating an apple
and it flies right out of her hand
but I manage to catch it before it lands in the dirt
which is pretty impressive.
Our school should have security cameras
so they can record such brilliant acts of athleticism.
I mumble 'sorry' to Laura
but she may have heard 'snotty'.
How can one girl produce so much runny stuff?
I reckon it's all the fruit she eats.
Can't be healthy for you, can it?

Laura grabs me by the arm.
Grabs me!
I'm about to punch her, of course,
but I remember what Mr Hume
said about violence.
Well, I don't actually
but he goes on about violence

every week at assembly.
I reckon he watches too much television.
So I don't punch Laura.
I wait until she wipes her nose on a hankie
and rubs the apple on her shirt,
in case of boy germs, I guess.
But she doesn't say anything.
She just holds my arm.
I say, 'What?'
I put on one of those dumb expressions,
like people do on TV game shows
when they've won a new washing machine
and can't believe it and are waiting for the host,
the guy with the shiny hair and even shinier suit,
to tell them, for the third time,
that, yes,
they've won something to wash clothes with.
Can you believe people get excited
about doing the laundry?
Anyway, Laura wipes her nose, again,
and says, 'Forget it.'
That's all.
Forget what?
At that very moment the bell rings.
I turn and start running to the circle of kids.

And you know what?

I was too late.

For the rest of the afternoon in class
all I heard were whispers from Cameron,
Pete and Alex
about what I'd missed.

Do you know what it was?

Nah.

Me neither!

LAURA

I don't know why I grabbed Mick,
it was an impulse.
I'll check the dictionary when I get home.
Impulse is the word I'm searching for, I'm sure.
Mum says I'm like that.
Unpredictable.
Just for a second, today,
when I grabbed Mick Dowling's arm,
I wanted to ask him why
he looks at me funny all the time,
ask him straight out.
He'd have to say something?
And then I'd know why the kids in class,
don't say anything to me.
They act like I'm not here.
A vacant chair in the third row.
Someone to push in front of in the canteen line.
The only time they seem to know I'm around
is when they're making jokes about me.
At least, I think that's what they're doing?

Impulse.

To act on initial emotion. On first thought.

Yep.

That's why I grabbed Mick's arm.

But you can't ask people questions like that.

They freak out and reckon you're a total nutjob.

I don't really care what they think

but, the truth is,

Mick wouldn't have answered anyway.

He would have told me to wipe my nose.

Snotty!

Hasn't he ever heard of hayfever?

The bell rang and I walked slowly to class.

I sat down, closed my eyes

and waited for the afternoon.

MR KORSKY

It happens once a year, without fail,
a few weeks after school begins.
A girl screams from down in the corner of the oval.
You can tell how close she came
to stepping on the poor thing
by just how loud she yells.
Usually it slithers away before anyone else notices
and the girl gets to tell the story
of the two-metre monster for the rest of term.
But sometimes, like today,
it's just too hot and the snake can't hear anyway
so no amount of yelling and hollering
is going to bother him.
He just lies there in the sun,
head up, just slightly,
feeling whatever breeze he can,
with the whole school gathering around
at a safe distance.
These kids are smart enough not to go too close,
except maybe Mick Dowling.
As I walk through the crowd I notice he's not here.
That's a blessing.

It's a red-bellied black,
who looks kind of sleepy,
so I get the children to move well back,
to give the young fellow the idea
that heading over into the saltbush might be wise.
The trick is not to do anything silly
like stamping on the ground close to them.
He's likely to strike then.

Just wait.

I keep talking to the children
about how snakes swallow their food
and how much venom it takes to kill a person.
They all listen to me
but keep their eyes on the snake.
And pretty soon, the bell goes
or the snake slithers away
and we all go back to doing
what we're supposed to.
I know where he's going.
Down to the river to have a swim.
Just like some of the boys in Year Six do,
at lunchtime,
even though they're not allowed.

I worry about the boys doing that,
but I remember that's what I did
when I was their age.
A swim in summer.
Who can resist that?

RACHEL

After the excitement
of the snake at lunchtime,
Ms Arthur
decides to play our favourite
two words game.
She elaborately writes
POOKIE ALEERA
on the whiteboard
and everyone wriggles uncomfortably
in their chair.
Cameron whispers,
'Never heard of him.'
Mick adds, 'Or her?'
Selina says, 'Or it?'
And then I understand,
so I quickly raise my hand and say,
'A chicken cooked in a *Pookie* sauce!'
Everyone giggles.
Cameron adds,
'A steam-powered toilet seat.'
Ms Arthur smiles,
nodding encouragingly.

Pete says, 'Harry Potter's Italian cousin!'

Laura adds, 'An eighties pop band!'

Selina, 'The woman who invented ping-pong!'

Alex, 'A fish that walks on water.

No, a fish that swims on land!'

Mick, 'A car that can go from zero to sixty

in two seconds.'

It goes on like this for the next few minutes

everyone throwing in silly suggestions

until Cameron raises his hand

and says,

loudly, of course,

'Pookie Aleera is your boyfriend, Ms!'

and everyone laughs,

even Ms Arthur.

PETE

A few weeks before he died
Grandpa told me a story
about a man in jail
who had no friends
except the pigeons and doves
who came to his window
each afternoon
to eat the scraps of food he'd offer,
a piece of fruit,
a bowl of water
and, pretty soon,
the birds were tame enough
to let the man reach through the bars
and touch their beating chests.
The man would whisper his sorrow
of all he'd done wrong
the crimes he'd committed
the hurt he'd caused.
Grandpa said
when the birds had finished eating
they'd fly away
and with them went the man's guilt

for all the bad things he'd done in his life.
Grandpa said the birds
saved that man's life,
so every day
before leaving home
I pick an apple
from the tree in our garden
and I take it to school
and leave it lodged in the tree branch
for the birds
and for Grandpa.

SELINA

As soon as we finish roll call this morning
Cameron raises his hand
but before he can speak
Ms Arthur picks up her phone from the desk
and says,
'What's your mobile number, Cameron?'
'0418816928, Ms.'
Ms Arthur presses the numbers
and
all of a sudden
the tune of 'Jingle Bells' sounds
from somewhere under Cameron's desk.
Ms Arthur smiles,
'Where's your phone, Cameron?'
Cameron reaches into his pocket
and holds up his phone,
it's Christmas time in March!
Ms Arthur stops her call and asks,
'I thought your phone was missing?'
Cameron says,
'That's what I wanted to tell you, Ms.
I found it . . . and I've given it a name.'

Everyone looks at Cameron
until Mick asks,
'What's it called?'
'Mr Nokia!'
Ms Arthur interrupts our giggles,
'Cameron, can you switch Mr Nokia to silent
and return it to your pocket, please?'
I wave at Cameron's phone and say,
'Bye, Mr Nokia.'
Cameron jiggles his phone
and says, in a mechanical voice,
'Bye, children.'

RACHEL

It's this thing we do.
A few of us,
at lunchtime, under the cherry tree,
near where Mick jumps over the fence
to sneak to the river,
even if he's not allowed.
He just shrugs and does it anyway.
Sometimes when he comes back to school
just before bell-time
he almost lands right in the middle of us.
He leans back against the fence
and listens to me and Selina
and Pete and Cameron
and Alex, of course,
talking about school and the weekend
or what we plan to do this afternoon,
or on Saturday night if our parents
let us visit each other.
Sometimes we take a vote
on what we're going to do next week,
as a group,
something special like bring in my DVD player

to watch a movie at lunch.
Or listen to music,
with everyone choosing one song.
Or bring in photos of when we were young,
the most embarrassing photos we can find.
Mick wouldn't be in that.
He said every photo is embarrassing.
Alex brought in a photo
of when he was a baby . . . wearing only a nappy!
He turned bright red when the others laughed.

It's my lunchtime gang.
My true friends.
The people I trust.

LAURA

There's a garden seat that Mr Korsky built
and he placed it under the gum trees
in the far corner of the schoolyard
away from the playground
and the classrooms and the canteen
and the bike racks
and the Principal's office
and the netball goals
and the library.
It's shady and cool here
and the grass doesn't grow
because the trees don't let in enough light.
Mr Korsky built the seat with old timber
and he painted it pale green,
the same colour as the trees,
and on the top rail of the seat
he carved the date he placed it in the shade
and every lunchtime
as soon as the bell rings
I race to my schoolbag for my sandwich
and I run up here and sit down
alone

and I watch everyone else
and I wish I could thank Mr Korsky
for making this seat
and for putting it here
away from the rest of the school.

MICK

I got named school captain.
Me and Selina.
And I'm captain of the football team
and the cricket team
and the other kids always ask me what I think
whenever something happens at school.
They reckon I'm a leader.
And Mum and Dad
trust me with the tractor
and the quad bike
and Dad knows I'll come home
straight after school
during harvest and I'll work until dark
and get up at first light and work some more.
Jacob follows me round the farm
and I can see he tries to do the things I do,
even if it's something stupid
like jumping off a shed roof.
And I get good marks in school
even though I don't try too hard
because I'm not going anywhere
other than this farm

and everyone in town knows that
but still they expect heaps from me.

And that's why when I get into trouble
and Mr Hume gives me one of his lectures
and reminds me of my duty
as school captain
and he shakes his head
as if he would have voted differently
if he had a choice.
That's when it takes all my effort
to stand there and not say a word,
in his office,
waiting for the lecture to end
so I can go back to class
where
all my true friends are.

RACHEL

It comes just before school finishes.
We hear it rumbling in the west
and Ms Arthur stops writing on the whiteboard,
looking nervously out the window.
Alex raises his hand and says,
'It's not a truck, Ms. Just a big storm.'
She asks Alex to shut all the windows in the library
and I stammer,
'Can I . . . can I help him, Ms?'
She nods and the two of us
race to the library,
Alex closes all the windows on the left side
and I take the right.
But before heading back to class,
Alex asks me to follow him
down to the flame tree by the back fence.
We watch the storm approaching,
like God's fists hammering down.
The purple clouds roll in,
the lightning crackles over the hills
and the sheep huddle near the saltbush,
but still we wait.

A storm takes its own good time.
When all we can hear is thunder
and our own breathing
we race each other back to class.
Everyone is crowding around the window.

The first drops kick up the dust
and batter the iron roof
and then it all goes silent,
just for a moment,
as if the storm is taking one huge breath,
before the rain, in angry waves,
dumps on the school
and the sheep paddocks
and the wheatfields
and everyone in the room cheers
except Mick who puts two fingers to his mouth
and whistles loud enough to crack the glass.

I can picture Dad and Mum
sitting on the verandah.
Mum's pouring a pot of tea
and Dad's slowly stirring in the sugar.

I can see the grin on his face from here.

CAMERON

My mum has these sayings
which I really like, but
I just don't understand.

When I'm having trouble
with a maths equation for homework
and she finds another way
of getting the correct answer,
she always laughs and says,
'There's more than one way to skin a cat.'
With a razor blade?
Or her lady shaver?
Or the sheep shears?
And why would you want to do that anyway?
Cats aren't sheep with woolly warm coats.
Seeing Rusty, the town tomcat, naked
would be quite a sight!

Late last night Mum said,
'Don't burn your candle at both ends',
when I was falling asleep while watching a video.
I spent all morning

trying to light a beeswax candle at both ends.
I dripped wax all over my fingers,
singed the hair on my wrist
and wasted lots of matches.
You *can't* burn a candle from both ends.
That's what Mum should say!

RACHEL

It's still raining lightly
when I get off the school bus
and I run,
slopping through the puddles
with the schoolbag over my head
until I reach the farm gate
where I hear music,
old-fashioned music,
coming from the front room
and
in the middle of the yard
is Dad, dressed in his overalls,
and Mum, in a summer dress,
and they're dancing,
arm in arm,
slowly around the garden.
When they see me
Mum giggles
and Dad waves for me to join them,
'Lovely weather, isn't it, Rachel?'

SELINA

During roll call this morning
Ms Arthur calls all our names,
'Pete
Tiffany
Selina (me!!)
Mick
Alex
Cameron
(he answers in a loud voice)
Grace
Rachel
right through until
Alice Zachary,
the last person alphabetically,
but before she closes the roll book
she smiles, to herself,
then calls out,
'Mr Nokia?'
and, quick as a flash,
Cameron answers,
in his machine voice,

'Here, Ms Arthur,
at your service
in all emergencies!'

CONSTABLE DAWE

'Good morning, Class 6A,
as you may remember,
my name is Senior Constable Dawe . . .
yes, *Senior*,
no, I haven't changed my name,
remember, it's my rank.
No, senior doesn't mean old, young lady,
it means
I've been promoted.
Today I'm here to talk about water safety,
swimmer safety,
as I think someone suggested last time.
Can anyone tell me
what you should do before swimming?
Yes, find some water to swim in.
That would be helpful.
But what about lessons?
Yes, I know you have lessons every day,
I mean, *swimming* lessons.
Have you all had swimming lessons?
Good.
So we're all confident in water.

Does that mean we just dive into any water?
No, you can't dive into a glass of water,
everyone knows that, young man.
Yes, I'm sure your dad says
he could dive into a bottle of beer in this heat
but I don't think he means it literally, does he?
Class 6A, do we all just go and dive into the river?
Or the ocean?
Or even the municipal pool
when the council finally gets around to fixing it?
No, of course not.
What should you do before jumping in?
No, you shouldn't get your friend to video
your fantastic dive.
Yes, I'm sure you can dive very well
but it's not going to help if you land on a rock.
Yes, you probably would make it on
Australia's Funniest Home Videos
but damaging your skull
to get on television
is not very funny, is it?
Please, Class 6A!
Yes, thank you, young lady,
we should check the depth of the water
before diving.

Or maybe not dive at all,
just step carefully into the water.
Yes, like an old man into a bathtub, young lady.
And what are we wearing, Class 6A?

I'm sorry,
we've been through the underpants issue before,
I hoped you'd all forgotten.
We are wearing swimmers and a rash shirt.
And why are we wearing a rash shirt?
No, not to stop you from getting rashes.
To stop sunburn.
Which means what should we also be wearing?
Anyone?
Remember slip, slop, slap?
No,
it's not slip on a banana skin
slop on an ice-cream
and slap on a naked bottom.
I thought we'd made all the naked jokes last time.
Slip on a shirt, slop on sunscreen and slap on . . .
yes,
a hat.
Thank you, Class 6A.
That's enough for today.

Next time we're going to talk about bushfire safety.

Okay, bushwalker safety.

And koala safety, if you will.

No, not bunyip safety.

Bunyips don't exist.

No, they didn't all die in the bushfire.

They're . . .

they're . . .

I'll leave that question to your teacher.

Thank you, Class 6A.'

LAURA

Ms Arthur
leads us into the library
and says
we have ten minutes
to choose a book to borrow
and
we can choose any book we like
including the comics
or
a picture book
or
a graphic novel
or
even just a magazine
but, she says,
we're not allowed
to choose poetry.
She points to the back wall
where the poetry is filed
under non-fiction .821
and she repeats
any book but poetry.

When we line up
to leave the library
I notice
Selina, Mick, Alex,
Rachel, Pete
and even Cameron
have chosen poetry books.

Ms Arthur checks out
each book
without saying a word,
a satisfied look on her face.

MR KORSKY

It was against Health and Safety Regulations,
I'm sure,
so I waited
until all the children and teachers had gone home.
I carried the ladder to the tree
where someone leaves an apple for the birds.
I climbed the ladder
and nailed the wooden ledge,
half-a-metre square,
to the branch
coming out at right angles from the trunk,
and I placed
a few apples
some birdseed
and a bowl of water
to encourage the birds
and I figure
once the children see them
they'll toss their fruit scraps
onto the platform

and we can all enjoy the parrots
and rosellas
and galahs
for as long as summer holds.

RACHEL

There's a deserted house on Baxter's Hill
with an old grapevine growing on the porch
and hanging over the front door.
You can see the house from every part of town.
Whenever there's a lightning storm
most of us kids hope
that it strikes the house
and starts a fire
so the ghost has to find someplace else.
No one dares go near.
Mick boasted he walked up to the front gate once
but not even he's going inside.
Mr Baxter died a year ago
and no one found him for ages.
They say he was sitting on the lounge,
his head bowed slightly.
They buried him on his property
because that's what it said in his will
and no one in town
had the heart to go against that.
His grave is on the hill,
under the she-oaks

and when the wind blows through the leaves
it sounds like somebody moaning.
An old man howling
for food
or water
or help.
That's why nobody,
not even adults,
goes up to Baxter's Hill.

JACOB

All my family loves peas,
but we have different ways of eating them.
Dad scoops them
carefully
onto his fork
and leans in close to the plate
before gobbling them up.
Mum rolls her eyes
and then rolls her peas
across the plate
and onto a soup spoon,
she drinks her peas
and doesn't spill a drop!
Mick uses his fork
to stab one pea at a time
but occasionally he just misses
and the pea shoots across the table
and onto the floor
where Skip slurps it up.
One pea for Mick, one for Skip.

And me?
I use the best pea-eating thing
ever invented . . . my fingers!

MR KORSKY

The truth is me and Walter Baxter
were best mates, all through school and after,
when we both got married and had kids.
And pretty soon those kids had children.
In the blink of an eye and the tip of a hat
me and Walter were grey-haired old men
wondering how so many days can go missing.
Walter's children moved away
and mine stayed
and I didn't think much of it at the time
but something got into him,
losing that part of himself.
He'd visit me and the wife in the evening.
We'd sit under the lemon tree
and have a few drinks,
watching the honeyeaters in the grevilleas.

Walter visited for years
until my grandkids arrived
and they were always under our feet,
chasing each other
giggling and tumbling around on the soft grass.

Don't get me wrong,
I loved it.
So did the wife.
But, sometimes, I'd catch Walter
looking at them as they played
and I could hear the sigh building
from deep down.
No one knows what makes a man
or what breaks a man.
Anyway, after his wife died,
Walter stopped visiting.
Once a week I'd go up to his place
and we'd sit in his tatty kitchen
not saying much.
Around these parts there's nothing to talk about
if it isn't the weather or family.
How long can you talk about the heat?
Or the wind?
So I went every fortnight instead.
Just two old blokes
staring out the window
listening to blowflies at the screen door.
The house was falling down
and Walter was too.
I did what I could,

bringing lamingtons the wife had baked,
helping him fix the shutters against the wind,
nailing the floorboards
where age and warp had taken their toll.
Once a fortnight wasn't enough.
I knew it.

When they found my friend,
I can't tell you how that made me feel.

SELINA

Cameron swears he saw
Ms Arthur at the grocery store
with a man wearing a red T-shirt, black jeans,
and a ponytail
and Cameron says
they were holding hands
as they walked along the footpath
and jumped into a green sports car,
and yes, we know,
Ms Arthur drives a blue Hyundai to school
and Cameron
tried to follow them
except the sports car
was faster than his bicycle
but he guessed
they were going to Dexter Street
where Ms Arthur lives,
so he took the short cut
across Harpers Paddock
and arrived just in time
to see them walking up the stairs
to her front door

and he couldn't resist,
he yelled,
'POOKIE ALEERA'
and
the ponytail man
looked around
so Cameron jumped behind a tree.
Cameron swears that proves
Pookie Aleera is Ms Arthur's boyfriend!

But, just as we all agree,
Rachel asks,
'Cameron, when you yelled out,
did Ms Arthur look around too?'
And Cameron says,
'Sure. I yelled so loud
everyone in the street turned around,
even Mr Hobbs the postman.'

And we all groan.

RACHEL

All morning on the Smart Board
Ms Arthur showed us paintings
of wheatfields
and churches
and cafés
and starry swirling nights
and bowls of fruit
and lots of paintings of the artist
because
Ms said
he was so poor he couldn't afford models
and fruit was cheap
and wheatfields were free
and Ms said
you pronounced his name, Van Gogh,
like *Fen Hoch*
not *Van Goff* or *Van Go*
and she told us he cut off his ear
and went to a place
where people with mental illness go
and Mick said,
'You mean the pub?'

and everyone laughed
even though
cutting off your ear didn't sound very funny
and we voted twenty-eight to nil
in favour of his paintings
and Ms said she'd seen the real paintings
in art galleries
and they were
'explosions of colour'
and
'the work of a genius'
and I thought maybe
he cut off his ear
because those explosions
had come out of his tortured mind
and landed on a canvas
and maybe
if he was really poor
and the people in the hospital
wouldn't let him paint
wouldn't let him do what he had to do
it made him mad enough
and angry enough
to hurt someone
and he couldn't hurt someone else

so he hurt himself.
I stared at his paintings for ages
and wondered what it would be like
to have all that going on inside your head.

CAMERON

The score was eight–eight
in our lunchtime soccer game
and Mick was doing his best
to win it for our team
dribbling down the wing
beating two defenders easily
before crossing it perfectly
for me
to take the biggest air swing in my life
and land flat on my back
in the dirt
and no one laughed
but no one cheered either
because the ball went out for a goal kick
and by the look on Mick's face
(even though he tried to hide it)
I was sure I'd lost the game
there and then.

There's only one minute and
(quick check of my watch)
twenty-two seconds

before the bell rings
for the end of lunch
and suddenly
I know just what to do.
I look across and see Rachel, the bell-ringer,
is checking her watch as well
when Mick gets the ball on the halfway line
so I run
not towards goal,
no air swings this time,
I sprint to the school verandah
as fast as my legs can go
and I leap the stairs two at a time
and peek into the staffroom
to check no one is leaving
then I reach for the school bell
and lift it carefully
holding the bell steady to stop it clanging
and I hide between the banksia hedge
and the office building
when Rachel runs towards the verandah
as Mick dribbles past Pete and Alex
and Rachel reaches the desk
where the bell should be
ready to ring it for the end of lunchtime

and that's when Mick beats the last defender
and curls a beautiful shot
into the top corner of the goal
for the winner
and everyone races to congratulate him
while I stand up from behind the hedge
and call to Rachel
that I've found the bell,
someone must have hidden it
to make lunchtime even longer
and who'd do something like that?
Rachel giggles and rings it
as loud as she can
while I run back to the oval
with Mick saying,
'Did you see it, did you see it?'
over and over again.

LAURA

You'd think everyone would know about it,
but each day it's the same.
All of Class 6A walk past the bushes,
talking and laughing on the way back from lunch.
I always wait to be last in line,
so I can rub my hands, just lightly,
along the top of the lavender,
purple thick with flowers.
Mr Korsky told me about it one morning
when Mum dropped me at school too early
and there was nobody else there.
He even let me trim some of the plants
with his clippers.
I think he still has a bad back
after saving Jacob's life.
He says he rubs his hands on the plants
first thing every morning
and before he goes home at night.
He says whenever he's upset,
or worried,
he just lifts his hands close to his nose
and lets the perfect aroma

take his troubles away.
I spend all afternoon in class
my chin in my hands
enjoying the smell
not worrying about a thing.

SELINA

It's a stinking hot day
and everyone is exhausted after lunch
and we're all slouched at our desks
while Ms Arthur
fans herself with a magazine
and no one wants to do school work
so Ms Arthur says
we'll have one super-quick
maths competition
and then we can all read
whatever we like
for the rest of the afternoon.
Ms Arthur says,
'Tell me the total of
six plus
five plus
eight plus
two plus
four plus . . .'
and Cameron
raises his hand
and says, 'Twenty-five!'

before Ms Arthur has asked him
and she says,
'I haven't finished yet, Cameron.'
A book is sitting on Cameron's desk, waiting.
Ms Arthur says,
'Right, nine plus
four plus
ten plus
three plus
seven plus . . .'
and Cameron
raises his hand
and says, 'Fifty-eight!'
and everyone groans
because we all know he's correct
but Ms Arthur hasn't finished
so she ignores the answer
and keeps going,
'. . . six plus
eleven plus
eight plus
two plus . . .'
Cameron says, 'Eighty-five!'
'. . . nine plus
twelve plus

three plus . . .'
Cameron says, 'One hundred and nine!'
'. . . two plus
ten plus
eleventy-seven plus . . .'
Ms Arthur smiles,
'. . . two trillion plus
one plus . . .'
and Cameron says,
'Two trillion, one hundred and twenty-two
and eleventy-seven, Ms!'

And, finally,
Ms Arthur says, 'Correct'
and tells us all
to spend the rest of the afternoon
reading.

ALEX

Me and Rachel wait until the weathervane
at school
is turning so fast
Mr Korsky has to take it down from the verandah.
Rachel winks at me in class and I nod.
After school we both ride our bikes
up to the Gap, just outside of town,
where the main road cuts between Baxter's Hill
and the abandoned apple orchard.
No one could grow fruit this far out
without irrigation
but legend has it, they tried for years
and one day after a huge dust storm,
the owners packed everything into their truck
and left town, never to return.
They say all the kids raced out here
and collected what was left of the shrivelled fruit
and the town had apple pies for weeks after.
Now there's nothing but a few withered trees
and a barn with half the roof missing.
Me and Rachel leave our bikes at the fence
and climb the rusty gate,

running into the breeze to the top of the rise,
opposite Baxter's Hill.
There are two huge granite boulders here
that shelter you from the wind.
We lean against the warm rocks
our heads tilting back to the sky
and spend all afternoon counting the clouds.
We don't say much
the wind is howling around us
and we're too busy keeping count.
I like the feel of Rachel's hand next to mine
but I don't tell her that.

LAURA

Every night, I open my diary
and write a few words before bed.

A self portrait –
crooked teeth jumbled hair
wears dresses, long and billowing, bright orange.
Eats sandwiches of salami, tomato sauce and pepper
washed down with juice
that Mum blends every morning
grinding carrots, beetroot, ginger and apple,
I sing loud over the noise.

A freckle under my T-shirt
near my bellybutton
like a friend, keeping me company.

Or sometimes I make a list of wishes –
a pony, black with a white blaze
or
a bicycle, with streamers
and a carry basket up front
for my cat . . .

which I don't have,
another wish.
An iPad
with my Facebook site
visited by friends
leaving me messages
and invites
and photos
and jokes
and videos
and
back to the real world
where I watch Mick and his gang
laughing at something funny.
Cameron rolling around
his face bright red
and Rachel looking misty-eyed at Alex
and Alex trying not to notice
and not one of them looks my way
they are alone
together
I'm alone
by
myself.

JACOB

Tonight is Mum and Dad's
wedding anniversary
and they want to go to the pub.
They don't want to leave
me and Mick at home
but Mick promises Mum
he'll ring her mobile if there's a problem
and he won't let me
burn the house down
or
flood the bathroom
or
let the chickens inside the house
but
luckily Mick doesn't promise Mum
that we won't climb onto the roof.
So ten minutes after they go,
we climb out the bedroom window,
Mick holding my hand tightly
like I'm just a kid.
We lean back against the chimney

and start counting the stars,
Mick calls each number out loudly,
we're up here for hours,
'152,153,154 . . .'
'Mick?'
'Yeah.'
'What do you reckon Mum and Dad
did before we were born?'
'Dunno. I wasn't here. 155,156,157 . . .'
'Mick?'
'Yeah.'
'How far away do you reckon the stars are?'
'One hundred million light years . . . or more.
158,159,160 . . .'
'Mick?'
'Yeah.'
'Have you ever been on a plane?'
'Nuh.161,162,163 . . .'
'It must be like sitting on a star.'
'164,165,166 . . .'
'Mick?'
'Yeah.'
'Have you ever been on a submarine?'
'167, 168, 169 . . .'

'Mick?'

'Yeah.'

'Can I have a go at milking Delilah?'

ALEX

Late at night
when I can't sleep,
I tiptoe out to the back verandah
where Trudi, our pet kelpie, is waiting.
She whines quietly
and rests her head on my lap
when I sit on the couch beside her.
She can't sleep either.
Together we watch
the wind swaying the plum trees in a slow dance
and the moonshadows tilting across the yard.
The cattle low softly in the far paddock
and just as I'm about to nod off to sleep
the rooster crows one long loud cackle
like a skeleton rattling
that sends shivers down my back.
I check my watch.
It's midnight.
I hear Mum's voice from inside,
talking to herself,
'I swear if that bird keeps it up
we'll be having roast chicken for dinner!'

Trudi, me
and the man in the moon
smile
before drifting off to sleep.
The rooster keeps quiet.

JACOB

Mick says
Delilah's not going to be happy
because it's past her milking time,
she may not give us any milk
and I'm to do it just the way he says.
It's muddy in the barn,
lucky we've got gumboots.
Delilah bellows
which means *hello* in cow-talk.
I'm carrying the stool,
while Mick has a metal bucket
and a clean washcloth.
He pats Delilah gently
and says her name over and over
as he gets me to place the stool beside her
and he sits on it
and rests his head on her flank
and he reaches underneath
and washes her udder with the warm cloth,
all the time saying her name.
And when she's ready,
he stands and I sit on the stool

and Mick tells me to gently
just gently
squeeze
with my thumb and forefinger
and I ask him which is my fourth finger
and he says, '*Forefinger*, Jacob'
and holds up the one next to his rude finger!

I squeeze and pull
and nothing happens except Delilah
makes a grunting sound,
which is cow-talk for
get your hands off me, I reckon.
I'm squeezing too hard
or Delilah is too tired
and wants to sleep
but
just when I'm about to give up
I hear a splash in the pail
and I so much want to cheer
but
I don't want to scare Delilah.
I slowly keep squeezing
until I've done every teat
and pretty soon,

we have enough milk
for a glass each
and before we leave Delilah
I give her a big hug
around her neck,
well, as far as my arms will reach,
to thank her for the milk
and for not kicking me.
In the kitchen, Mick adds
two spoonfuls of Milo
to our glasses
and we have
a rich, warm, thick, real milkshake,
all thanks to Delilah
and my brother.

CAMERON

She can ride a bike faster than anyone,
I follow in her wake.
She cradles a lady beetle in her hand,
I wish I could hold it.
(Her hand not the beetle!)
She laughed for
two minutes and twenty-five seconds at lunch
but I didn't tell the joke.
On Mondays she wears a black beret,
I tell her it's my favourite colour.
On Tuesday she wears a red ribbon,
I tell her it's my second favourite colour.
On Wednesday her hair falls free.

She answered four questions correctly in class,
I answered three questions wrong.
She got voted onto the school council,
I got mumps and missed the election.
She is the only girl in the school football team,
I'm the only boy in the softball team.
She has a dog named Napoleon,
a cat named Louis,

four goldfish,
two chooks that lay eggs,
and a mouse called Roger.
I have a pet rock.
I had a pet rock
until Mum threw it away.
Mum didn't know it was a pet,
she said she was sorry,
went out to the garden
and brought me in another rock
but it was just a rock,
not a pet,
so I let it go home.

MICK

'I broke Charlie Deakin's cricket bat
by hitting it against a tree trunk
until the handle snapped.
It's true
but . . .
yes, sir,
no buts about it,
I'll take this note home to Mum and Dad
and I'll pay for his bat.
Yes, sir, I know
his dad is the only doctor in town
but . . .
yes, sir,
I'll apologise to Charlie.
I know I'm school captain
and I should set a good example
but . . .
yes,
I promise not to do it again, sir.'

And then I walked
slowly back to class

the note to my parents
in my pocket
and the memory of Charlie
with his brand new cricket bat
practising his hook shot
on the butterflies
swarming across the oval
killing five at a time
with each swing of his bat
before anyone arrived for school
this morning.

JACOB

At dinner –
chicken schnitzel, potatoes, beans and gravy –
Mum says to Mick,
'I'm very disappointed
that you'd do such a thing.'
Dad says,
'You'll work every afternoon
for an extra hour on the farm
to pay for his new cricket bat.'
Mick quietly and slowly eats his dinner.
Mum says,
'We expect better of you, Mick.'
Dad says,
'What on earth were you thinking?'

I can't take it any longer.
I say, 'Tell them about the butterflies, Mick.'
Mum says,
'Now is not the time, Jacob.'
Dad says,
'This is very serious, Jacob.
Your brother has . . .'

'Tell them, Mick, tell them,' I say
interrupting Dad, which I never do.
Dad looks angry and his face goes red
but I don't think it's sunburn
and he says,
'Jacob!'
I can't stop now,
so I say, in my loudest voice,
'He killed the butterflies!'
Everyone goes quiet
and I don't know where to look
so I stare at my dinner
for the longest time
until Dad says,
'Who killed what butterflies?'
'Charlie,' I say,
'with his cricket bat,
smashing hundreds of them.'
Mum and Dad look at each other
and now Mum's face is going red too
and then she gets up from her chair
and walks around the table to Mick
and she leans down close
and all of a sudden
Mick reaches out to hug her

and he buries his face
in her chest and sniffles
and Mum hugs him tightly
and Dad reaches across
and pats my hand,
'Thanks, Jacob.
We'll sort it out tomorrow.'
He coughs, nervously,
'We'll fix it, no worries.'

MICK

Before bedtime,
I go into Jacob's room
with my Lego plane,
the model with the jet engines
and plastic cockpit
where the yellow-headed pilot sits.
He has a weird moustache
and he's wearing a white helmet
as if he's expecting the plane to crash
and for years
Jacob has come into my room
and picked up the plane on my desk
and laughed at the scared, crazy pilot.
Tonight I place the plane
carefully on Jacob's bedside cupboard
and he sits up in bed and giggles,
'We're all gunna crash!'
I walk to the door and say,
'Goodnight, Jacob.'
He waves, laughing,
'We're all gunna crash!'

LAURA

I thought it would make Mr Korsky happy.
It took hours searching the internet
for just the right site
and I printed out recipes
of things I never knew you could make
from a plain old bush of purple flowers.
All he needed was a saucepan
and a stove or a barbecue.
I can picture him
cooking it up,
leaning over the bowl
smelling the perfume as it steams.
I bought a folder from the newsagent
and I put all the pages inside
and tied them with a purple ribbon.
This morning
I got Mum to drop me at school early,
before Mr Korsky arrived,
and I ran to the lavender bushes
and picked a single stalk,
held it up to my nose
and placed it in the folder.

I slipped the folder under his door
and calmly walked to the oval
to watch him, from a distance.

LAURA

I can't explain the feeling.
It's too big, overwhelming,
like the sky in summer.
He had a frown on his face
when he picked up the folder,
thinking Mr Hume
had slipped more work under his door.
And then he saw the stalk of lavender
and, I swear, I could see the wrinkles of a smile
stitched across his face.
He stood at the shed door
and read through every note I'd included.
He took the pencil he keeps in his top pocket
and added his own ideas to my notes.
There were a few kids around the playground now,
I had to be careful or else someone would notice.
When he finished he put the notes
back in the folder,
tied it with the same ribbon
and walked into his shed,
placing it on the top shelf above his bench,
where no one could reach it.

He came back outside,
the stalk still in his hands,
he held it up to his nose
and laughed,
it was the best laugh I'd ever heard.

MICK

I got to school earlier than usual.
I thought no one was around
until I saw Laura.
She seemed to be spying on somebody,
so I ducked behind a bottlebrush
and felt like a real fool.
She was watching Mr Korsky unwrap something.
A present?
Maybe it was her mum's acupuncture kit?
To help Mr Korsky with his bad back.
You wouldn't catch me letting someone
stick pins in my body
like I was a voodoo doll!
Laura wandered around the schoolyard
watching Mr Korsky.
She almost walked into a tree
she was so involved.
And when Mr Korsky laughed,
booming loud,
I could see the smile on Laura's face.
Two of them,
sharing a secret.

MICK

I don't get it.
Mr Hume comes up to me at recess
and says he got a phone call from Dad
and they agreed
I don't have to pay for Charlie's cricket bat.
The school has a few spare bats
and one of those
will be given to Charlie
to replace the bat I smashed.
Then he coughs
as if he hadn't wanted to say that word,
smashed,
and he looks like he wants to say
something else
but he can't quite manage it
so he coughs again
and says
we should all just forget,
this unfortunate incident,
that's what he calls it.
And as he walks away
the question comes to me . . .

what if Charlie
uses the new bat,
the school bat,
to practise on the butterflies again?

ALEX

My Grandpop
leans against the counter
in the barber shop
while Mr Chambers
carefully snips the hair
from around my ear.
Grandpop says,
'In my day, Alex,
my dad would take to me
with sheep shears
and, Bob's your uncle,
I'd be shorn true
and booted outdoors to work.'
Mr Chambers laughs
and carefully snips at my fringe.
Grandpop says,
'In my day
us kids didn't have iPads
and iPhones and iPoodles,
or whatever they're called.
We had a bat, a ball and a bike.
Too many gadgets, too much . . .'

Grandpop's mobile phone beeps
with a text message.

He moves away from the counter
and pulls it out of his overalls
and starts to text back.
Mr Chambers sprays a mist of water
on my hair
and snips on top.
Grandpop finishes texting
and slips the phone into his pocket.
'Now, what was I saying?' he asks.
Mr Chambers winks at me and says,
'Football, you were talking about footy.'

LAURA

Ms Arthur said,
'It's not
pop stars
or actors
or supermodels
or celebrities
or millionaires
or sports stars
who are lucky and special . . .
it's
someone who has
a partner
a friend
a parent
who loves them.'
I remember her saying that
when I'm walking home from school
and I see Mum,
waving to me
from the front verandah,
waiting to take me to Johnson's Café

for a strawberry thickshake,
to celebrate
her one day off work.

CAMERON

Mum was mixing gooey stuff in a bowl
when I woke up
and I thought it looked like fun
so I asked her if I could help,
you know, stirring it around
and maybe I could lick the bowl
when she finished?
She took off her apron,
handed it to me
and helped me tie it behind my back.
I felt kind of silly wearing it
but I could wipe my hands on it
whenever they got sweaty
from all the stirring I did
with the wooden spoon.
It took a lot of mixing before Mum was happy
with the gluggy goo in the bowl
and we added some shredded coconut
and then she let me stir it some more
while she spread a thin smear of butter
on a baking tray.
She checked the oven was the right temperature

while I dolloped lumps of the mix on the tray.
She showed me how to press them flat
with the palm of my hand
and then let me lick the bowl.
We slid the tray into the oven
and set the timer for twenty minutes.
I sat in front of the stove
eating my Weet-Bix
waiting
smelling
watching.
When Mum tipped the biscuits out on the rack
I couldn't resist
even though they were so hot
I juggled one like a cricket ball
before taking a huge steaming bite.
Delicious!
Mum let me take ten,
yes, ten Anzac biscuits
to school
to share at lunchtime
with the gang.
My biscuits I'd baked.

MICK

It came to me
when we were eating Cameron's biscuits.
Or 'biting the bikkies' as Selina joked.
They were sweet and crunchy
and smelt like warm butter.
I didn't believe Cameron had baked them
until I saw him blush
when we all said how good they were.
And it came to me,
out of nowhere,
this thought,
this idea I can't get out of my head.

In class all afternoon
I stare out the window thinking of nothing else,
except this single simple idea.
Only it's kind of hard to explain,
that's why I keep turning it over in my head.
It's got to do with Cameron and his biscuits
and how we all loved scoffing them
and
how it made Cameron feel good sharing,

and watching us eat them!
And I remembered yesterday morning,
Laura watching Mr Korsky laugh,
and the look on her face.
That's when I realised,
it all made sense
and I almost fell off my chair
which happens a bit during maths
but that's because I'm usually falling asleep.
Not this time.
This time it was my brilliant idea.
Laura was happy doing something for Mr Korsky.
Mr Korsky was happy
with whatever it was she did.
Cameron was happy sharing Anzacs
and we were all very, very happy eating them
and
and
and
that's when I knew what to do.
What to say tomorrow at lunchtime
to the gang
who think I'm a leader
when I'm not
but this time

maybe I can make a suggestion
and we can all try my idea
for a week
and see what happens.

CAMERON

I admit it,
I don't usually ride home on Dexter Street,
where Ms Arthur
just happens to live
but
it's a nice street
with no dogs to chase me
and there's a scatter of gravel
where I can practise skids on my bike
and I can't help it
if I glance,
just casually,
into Ms Arthur's yard
and I'm not really looking for the sports car
or Pookie Aleera,
the ponytail man,
but, I swear,
if he comes out into the yard
I'm going to wave and call out his name
again.
Maybe I'll stop and shake his hand,
introduce myself,

'Hi, I'm Cameron . . .
and you're . . .'

The old lady at the corner house,
weeding her garden
waves to me
every time I pass.
I wave back,
keeping a lookout for Pookie.

ALEX

On Baxter's Hill
the wind bangs the door
of the ghost house
as Rachel and I
stand outside
staring into the lonely yard
where the dog chains
are rusting in the stinkweed
and every window pane is broken
and a piece of roofing iron
flaps like a wounded bird.
The gate creaks
as Rachel opens it
and steps through
reaching behind for my hand.
A crow lands on the chimney
and squawks,
as if to scare us away.
Rachel whispers,
'Do you think Mr Baxter would mind?'
I hope his ghost
is as hard of hearing as he was.

The blade grass prickles my legs,
please don't let there be snakes,
or spiders or rats.
We're two steps away from the verandah
when the door opens
with the wind
and I can see
all the way down the hallway
to the kitchen
where one chair stands beside a table
waiting,
and Rachel says, 'Alex'
as we reach the front door
and just as I'm about
to step into the house
the wind blows hard
and slams the door
like a hammer.
Rachel screams
or was it me?
We both turn and run
and don't stop
until we reach the rock ledge
on the hill overlooking the ghost house,
the sweat on the back of my neck

chills my body
and Rachel says, 'Alex'
and I answer, 'Yes'
and she giggles nervously,
'Can we not go inside, please?'
We both stare
at Mr Baxter's house
and the door opens slowly
as if daring us to try once more
and I say to Rachel,
'Okay, let's not.'

SELINA

Today is mufti day
and we've all brought in a gold coin donation
for World Vision and the starving children
all over the world
and
everyone has worn their favourite clothes.
Most of the boys wear footy jerseys and jeans
and
the girls wear riding pants and boots,
but
the two best outfits are
Ms Arthur
who wears her old school uniform from Year Twelve,
'Too many years ago,' she says.
She looks funny in a tartan skirt
and a white blouse with matching socks!
And Cameron wears
black jeans and a red T-shirt
with his hair tied back in a ponytail.
On his T-shirt
he's written in black texta,
'Who is Pookie Aleera?'

When Ms Arthur sees him,
she giggles and says,
'Nice haircut, Cameron.
I like a man with a ponytail.'

Cameron blushes,
redder than his T-shirt!

MICK

When we sit together at lunch today
Alex asks Cameron
if he's got any more biscuits.
We all look eagerly at Cameron
who sadly shakes his head.
No one says anything for a minute,
all of us thinking of their steaming buttery taste.
'I've got an idea,' I say, nervously.
Pete answers quickly,
'Anything to do with food?'
'Not exactly.
But it could be, if you want.
It's the best idea I've ever had.'
Everyone leans forward
and I wish I hadn't said that.
'Well, maybe the second best . . .'
I wait a few seconds,
just to be sure everyone is listening.
I keep my voice low,
'We all agree, for one week,
to be nice to everybody . . .
and see what happens.'

I sit back and wait.

Rachel looks at Alex
who looks at Pete
who looks at Cameron
who looks at Selina
who stares at me and says,
'So what's your idea?'
'That's it,' I say.
'We be nice to everyone.
Just for a week.'
Rachel scratches her head,
'But aren't we nice all the time?'
Cameron looks at his empty lunch box,
'I reckon a better idea
is to make another batch of biscuits!'
Selina giggles, 'Yeah, now that's real nice!'
I say,
'No. No. No.
You don't get it.
I mean *really really* nice.
Let's go out of our way
to do something . . . special,
for someone else
and see what happens.

Just for a week.'
Cameron laughs and says,
'Great idea, Mick. Brilliant!'
Everyone looks at Cameron.
I say, 'Thanks.'
Cameron giggles,
'That's okay, I was just being nice.'
Everyone laughs.
Even me.
But we all agree
to give it a try.
For one week.

MICK

I should make the first move,
it being my idea.
So before the bell rings
for the end of lunch,
I leave the gang
and walk to the bench where Laura sits,
alone, of course.
As I sit down she closes the book she's reading
her eyes looking everywhere all at once
except at me.
I'm sure her knees are shaking,
just like mine.
I stretch my legs, look at the hole in my right shoe,
even whistle a little
just to show I'm relaxed
and exactly where I want to be
except
I have no idea what to say
to Laura.
I can hardly ask how the nose is running, can I?
Two statues on a seat, that's us.
I glance at my watch,

three minutes until the bell.
I don't know what to do with my hands
so I put them under my legs
to keep them from waving around
like a lost puppet.
Laura turns to me and says
in a quiet voice,
'Is this a dare?'
I look quickly towards the gang
afraid they're all laughing
or making rude gestures.
'No. No way, Laura.
I just . . .'
I haven't really thought this through, have I?
She says,
'I don't need someone to sit beside, you know.'
She holds up the book
as if to say she has a friend.
'Yeah. I mean, no.
I . . . I thought you might like to sit
with the rest of us.'

What am I saying?

Laura looks from me to the gang
and back to me.
She's about to answer
when the bell rings
and I jump up
eager to get away
but
that makes me look foolish
so I sit down again,
as Laura stands
and when she looks at me
I notice the pity
as if she doesn't want to hurt my feelings.
All she says is,
'Thanks.'
She turns to walk to class
and I call out,
'Maybe tomorrow then.'
She doesn't look around.
Tomorrow is Saturday.

LAURA

Mum says,
'If in doubt,
count to ten before answering.'
But when Mick invited me
to join his gang,
I wanted to spring up
and shout yes!
But Mum's voice crept in
and I waited
and thought about it.
Why?
Why now?
Why me?
I didn't like the answers
whispering in my head.
I looked across at his gang.
They were all doing their best
not to look this way
but I couldn't trust myself
or them
or anything except the book in my hands.

Why did he pick on me?
I'm happy on the bench,
it's my spot,
my place.
Why did he pick on me?

MICK

In class,
my mind plays gymnastics.
She likes a book more than me?
She likes a hard wooden seat
better than the grass
and the gang?

Ms Arthur wrote twenty questions
in her flowing handwriting on the board.
I answered them,
easy,
one after the other,
in my notebook.

I looked at Laura
sitting in the third row
and I asked my own questions,

and spent the afternoon
not answering them.

CAMERON

I've just switched on my new iPad
that Grandma bought me,
when Dad knocks on my door
and asks me if I want to play
parisian rings in the backyard
and
I've just linked to a YouTube video
of these skater dudes doing half-pipes,
but I don't want to hurt Dad's feelings,
so I mumble about homework
and Dad says
we should play parisian rings instead
if he can suggest ten good reasons.
So I pause YouTube
and Dad holds up one finger:
'It's a beautiful sunny day outside.'
He holds up two fingers:
'It's . . . it's not raining',
which is really just the same reason as his first one,
but I don't say anything.
Three fingers:
'It's . . . it's more fun than an iPad!'

I frown.

He hasn't seen YouTube lately.

Dad's starting to look fidgety,

like I do in class when I don't know the answer

to a question Ms Arthur has just asked.

Four fingers:

'Your mother . . . won't play with me!'

We both giggle.

Dad relaxes.

Five fingers:

'We can't throw an iPad forty metres in the house!'

Six fingers:

'I'm bored!'

Seven fingers:

'I need to lose weight.'

Eight fingers:

'My dad threw a cricket ball with me

when I was your age!'

Nine fingers:

'I need an excuse not to mow the lawn!'

Ten fingers:

'Did I mention it was a beautiful day?'

I turn off my iPad.

Me and Dad play parisian rings
until it gets dark
and we beat our record
of one hundred and fifteen throws
without dropping it once,
when Mum calls out to Dad,
'Don't forget you promised
to mow the lawn today!'

PETE

After Sunday lunch,
Nan goes out to the garden
with a pair of scissors
and cuts a single flower
a rose
and she slowly walks
across the paddock to Grandpa's grave,
the flower in one hand
her walking cane in the other.
She sits on the cool granite
and places the flower in the vase
next to his headstone
then she sings Grandpa a song.
Nan's voice
floats on the wind,
as fragile as glass
and
as sad as loneliness
and Mum stops washing the dishes
and listens
from the kitchen window.

SELINA

Ms Arthur wears a football jersey to school
even though it isn't mufti day.
It has red and blue stripes
and when Cameron raises his hand
and asks the name of the team she supports,
Ms Arthur smiles
and instead of answering,
she asks Cameron and me to draw the curtains
on either side of the classroom
and she shows us a video on the Smart Board.
It's highlights of her football team
and Ms turns down the commentary
and tells us the story of their best player
who scores lots of goals in the video
and how when he was twelve years old
he could barely walk
because he had a growth hormone deficiency
(she writes it on the whiteboard).
No one would give him a chance
to do what he wanted
which was to play football
except this one club in Spain

that had a special school
that taught football differently than anywhere else
and the teachers saw this boy was special
and they accepted him into their family
and now
he's the most famous footballer in the world
who earns millions of dollars
and his name is Lionel Messi
and the club is FC Barcelona
and they're world champions
and Ms Arthur stops the video
and points to the logo on her shirt
which reads
UNICEF
and she tells us that
instead of taking money for sponsorship
like every sporting club in the world
Barcelona gives money
to the United Nations Children's Fund
and then she giggles
and bites her lip as if she wants to tell us
something else about them . . .
we wait . . .
and wait . . .
and finally, Cameron says,

'Come on, Ms, what else?'
And Ms Arthur giggles again
and says that the supporters of her team
are nicknamed 'Cules'
which in Spanish
is a rude word for bottom
or bum
because when the club started
their stadium was so old
that the supporters would sit
with their bottoms hanging over the rafters.
We all laugh
and, sure enough,
Cameron raises his hand
and says,
'Ms, I'd like to be a bum too!'

RACHEL

Monday lunchtime.
The gang sits in a circle,
each of us with a smile bigger than Uluru.
Everyone has a parcel on their lap,
except Mick,
who nervously looks towards Laura,
still on her seat.
Alex looks at me and says,
'You first.'
Everyone fumbles with their parcels,
all of us eager, at the same time.
I shake my head.
'Let's open them together.'
We've all spent the weekend
thinking
what to do
to be nice to each other,
Mick's idea.
All weekend.

Selina nods
and I count to three.
The five of us unwrapping together.

Nervous giggles.

Selina, Cameron, Pete, Alex and me,
everyone has the same surprise
which isn't a surprise at all.
Five batches of freshly baked biscuits.
Mick says,
'Mum was out of flour . . .'

We count them.
Seventy-four biscuits.
Too many to eat in a week of lunchtimes.
Alex puts the lid on his container and asks,
'What do we do?'

Silence.

Mick slowly grins.
He reaches across and lifts two from my cake tin.
I nod.
He says,

'Maybe Laura is hungry?'
He stands and takes a deep breath.
As he walks away, I understand.
I gather my tin and
ask Alex if he wants to make friends
with the Year Fours playing cricket.
Selina walks to the staffroom.
Pete says,
'Year Fives will eat anything, I reckon!'
And Cameron spies Jacob with the Infants,
adding, 'Jacob's always hungry!'

It's the best lunchtime I've ever had.
Me and Alex giving biscuits
to the sweaty kids in Year Four!

LAURA

I could smell the warm yeasty aroma
before he sat down
next to me
on Mr Korsky's seat.
He handed me one
without saying a word.
My first impulse was to say no.
No thanks.
My voice caught in my throat
as he held it nearer
and I took it quickly.
He took a big bite
and said,
with his mouth half-full,
'Rachel baked them. Not me.
If you're worried . . .
about food poisoning.'
I giggled.
Then I took a big bite to stop myself
from laughing at Mick Dowling
sitting beside me on the seat,
more nervous than me.

I chewed slowly
with my mouth closed
like Mum says I should.
'It's . . . delicious, Mick.'
I said his name,
like we're friends.
He looked at the half-eaten biscuit in his hands
as if it could tell him what to say next.
He smiled,
'I can get you another one . . . if you want?
Geez . . . I can get another fifty!'
I shake my head, quickly.
And then I decide what to do
when I get home this afternoon.
Chocolate crackles.
Mum's recipe.
For tomorrow.
For Mick
and his friends.

CAMERON

Me and Jacob
eat one biscuit each
just to make sure they taste okay.
They taste better than okay!
So we call the Kindy kids
playing on the monkey bars
and, pretty soon,
there are too many children to count
pleading for a biscuit
and I have no idea what to do,
the kids swarming like ants over a sugar bowl!
Jacob whispers into my ear,
'Half the size, half a biscuit.'
I give him the tin to hold
while I break each biscuit in half
and hand them
to the giggling kids
who don't seem to mind sharing.
When all the Infants have
gone back to the playground
and left me and Jacob
with an empty tin,

Jacob grins and says,
'Do you reckon, if I came over to your place,
you could teach me how to bake them, Cameron?'

CONSTABLE DAWE

'Good morning Class 6A,
hands up if you remember my name.
Good, that's everyone . . .
except the boy at the back.
Can anyone give him a hint, perhaps?
Yes, thank you for all pointing at the door.
Very imaginative,
my name is Senior Constable Dawe,
spelt D-A-W-E.
That's right,
still Senior.
There is no *Super* Senior rank, I'm afraid.
Today,
we're talking about bushfire safety,
but we agreed last time
to call it *bushwalker* safety.
Please don't mention bunyips.
When camping, what's the best way
to prevent a bushfire?
Yes, camp in your bedroom,
or in the backyard,
but what about in the bush?

What should you do with your camp fire?
Yes, have a big barbecue,
but afterwards?
Yes, of course,
eat all the sausages!
I mean after you've finished with the camp fire,
why are you giggling, young man?
What is *so* funny?
You've remembered how your dad
put out the camp fire,
well,
please share it with us all.
He what!
He did that on a camp fire!
I'm sorry, toilet humour is not appropriate.
Yes, even if it did extinguish the camp fire
but
a bucket of water from the river
would work just as well.
Now settle down, Class 6A,
we have established
that putting out the camp fire is important,
this giggling is really not getting us anywhere.

What happens if you're caught in a bushfire?

Yes, this time you *do* run like heck, young man.

But where?

Away from the fire.

Yes, very sensible and logical.

To the river . . . good.

To a patch of ground without grass or trees, yes.

No, not up a tree, young man.

You're not being chased by a bear.

Yes, I know bears don't exist in Australia.

Koalas aren't bears, young lady.

And being chased by a koala

is hardly life-threatening, is it?

Do not run uphill,

fires move faster uphill than down.

Look for a road or a gully without vegetation.

Yes, call the fire brigade, that's correct.

Who knows what number to call?

No, not 911,

that's in America, children.

Surely we know,

yes, of course, 000.

And tell the person, calmly, where you are.

No, screaming "I'm in a bushfire" won't help.

Try to locate a landmark.

Finally,
and I really don't want to go into this too much,
but what clothes should we wear
when walking in the bush,
and before anyone says it,
yes, underwear,
let's all have clean underwear on,
just in case.
What else, Class 6A?
No, swimmers are not necessary.
Yes, I know I said to run into the river,
but keep your clothes on this time,
to protect against the fire.
What should you always wear on your feet
when bushwalking?
Shoes.
Not thongs, not barefoot, but good leather shoes.
I'm sorry your mum doesn't wear leather
because she's vegetarian, young lady.
Yes, we all want to save the world, young lady,
each in our own way.
So, are we agreed, Class 6A,
while bushwalking,
wear good protective clothing,
and in a bushfire,

run towards a river
or open ground without vegetation,
and yes,
throw water on the camp fire.
Okay,
pee on a camp fire
if it makes you and your dad happy, young man!
Thank you Class 6A,
that's my last talk for this term.
It's been . . .
enlightening.'

LAURA

I put four cups of Rice Bubbles
in Mum's mixing bowl
sprinkle a dash of cocoa
and then more cocoa
and then even more because
too much chocolate is never enough.
I add a cup of icing sugar
and some melting rich Copha
the way Mum told me
when I rang her at work.
She asked me if I needed anything
and I suggested another packet of Rice Bubbles
just in case
my recipe turns into torture.
I mix everything together
for exactly fifteen minutes
until my arms ache.
I sprinkle coconut on top and mix again.
I wonder if Mick likes crackles?
Everyone likes crackles!
One good turn deserves another.
I spoon the mix into patty cake papers

and slide the tray into the fridge.
I sit in the kitchen
waiting for them to set
wishing
fridges had glass doors
so I could watch
and check
and hope
that they taste as good as they look.

CAMERON

I ring her mobile
and when she answers
I act surprised and say,
'Oh, hi, it's you!
I meant to ring Mick.'
And she says,
'Who is this?'
And I'm so nervous,
I answer, 'It's me.'
She giggles,
which is a start, I guess,
and says,
'Hello me,'
and I say, 'Hi' again,
just to be polite
and then we both giggle
and I say I was going to ask Mick
if he'd like to meet me down at the river
near the campground for a swim
and maybe have a thickshake
at Johnson's Café
and she says,

'I like thickshakes.'
And I blush bright red
but that's okay
because I'm hiding underneath our house
where I know I won't be seen
and I say,
'Why don't we meet in an hour?'
and she giggles again
and says,
'Sure.'
Then we both go silent
for a million minutes
until I say,
'Great, I'll see you then.'
And she says,
'See you then, *me*.'

JACOB

Me and Mick sit on the back verandah
watching our dog Skip chase the ball
every time Mick throws it,
no matter where he hurls it.
I didn't know Skip could swim so well.
Or Mick could throw the ball
all the way to the dam.
Mick keeps smiling to himself
and I know it isn't because Skip
gets soaking wet
and shakes dam water
all over us,
the easiest way to cool down in summer.
It's because of the biscuits,
Mick's brilliant idea.

Such a simple plan.
The tennis ball
is soaked with dam water
and Skip's spit,
but no matter how many times my brother
throws the ball

Skip chases it
and brings it back
to drop at our feet.

MR KORSKY

I drove my ute
up to Walter Baxter's place
on Monday afternoon
and I sat on the front verandah
looking out over the town
just like Walter and I used to do
when he was alive.
I poured a beer in two glasses
and drank from them both
until the sun drifted
behind the hills.
The window frames rattled in the wind
and I told Walter
all the news I could think of:
the footy team's win on Saturday,
the joy of the Parker's wedding,
how the council
opens the library on Thursday nights now,
and
I told Walter
how much I miss him.
Then I went to the ute

and lifted the lawn-mower out
filled it with two-stroke
and set to work on his yard.
The evening faded
and afterwards
I had another beer
with Walter
and admired the view.

CAMERON

I've been sitting
waiting
beside the river
for exactly twelve minutes
and thirty-two seconds
when I see her
riding across the bridge.
I pretend not to notice
and start whistling casually
except
I'm not a very good whistler
so I accidentally dribble
and blow a huge raspberry
which I quickly wipe on my sleeve.
I try humming instead
huuummmm hhuummm hhhuuummm.
'Hello, me,' she says.
'Oh, hi,' I answer.
'I knew it was you, me, who phoned,' she says.
I smile.
'Should I keep calling you *me*?' she asks.
'Cameron is fine,' I say.

'Hi, *Cameron is fine*,' she says, and giggles.
After a few minutes
of no one speaking
she asks,
'Can you whistle?'

RACHEL

Sometimes I wake
in the middle of the night.
A tree branch scratches at my window.
Dad snores like a broken kettle.
I know Mum is sleeping beside him
earplugs in place.
Our dog Maisy snuffles beside my bed.
She can't sleep either.
A breeze clinks the wind chimes
on the verandah
and then I hear it,
what I've been hoping for . . .
a barn owl hoots . . .
I scramble out of bed
and creep to the window.
Maisy whines.
Shhhh!
Maisy follows my eyes
and we both sit
wide awake
waiting
for the applause of wings

as the white-faced owl
circles high over our yard
like a delicate kite
before swooping into the paddock
and snatching up a fieldmouse
from the wire grass.
Maisy goes back to her blanket
and I climb into bed.
My clock glows midnight.
I close my eyes
and fly over the paddocks
with the owl
in the perfect moonlight
of my dreams.

LAURA

I'm not sure when
to give Mick the crackles.
Should I leave them on his desk
with a note from *anonymous*?
Or sneak them into his backpack
hanging on the verandah?
Maybe I'll just hand him the package
and walk away before he has a chance to say no.
The bell rings for class,
the crackles stay hidden in my bag.
At morning recess, I can't find Mick,
maybe he's hiding from me?
All morning in class I think of the crackles
and hope they're not melting.

At lunch I sit on my bench seat
the package of crackles on my lap
watching Mick and his friends
lazing against the back fence, laughing
and I know there's only ten minutes
until the afternoon bell
and I can't bear it any longer

so I take a deep breath,
and walk, knees knocking, hands shaking,
towards Mick and his gang.
Rachel sees me first and says, 'Hi'
and Mick looks up
and I get scared
so I casually toss the parcel
and luckily he's a good catch
and he laughs and says, 'Whoa!'
which is not a word,
not really, it's just a sound,
and I don't know what to say
so I turn and start to walk
back to my bench
where I belong
and Mick says, 'Laura'
he calls my name
so I turn back to him
and he unwraps the parcel
and everyone looks inside and laughs.
Cameron says, 'Not more biscuits!'
and Mick blushes,
I'm sure he blushes, and says,
'Sit down and help us eat them.'
He looks up at me and adds, 'Please?'

And then he makes a space
between him and Selina
and offers me the first crackle
and it tastes
as fresh and crisp and sweet
as friendship.

RACHEL

Ms Arthur said
at her last school
in the city
they didn't have
snakes in the playground
or children jumping off sheds
trying to fly.
She said
they didn't have summer storms
that threatened to wash away the town
or students who yelled and saluted
in answer to roll call
and they didn't have
butterfly swarms
or days so windy and hot
it was like teaching in an oven
and she didn't remember her city school
having a ghost house nearby
and the children swam in a heated pool
not in the river
and her last school didn't have
an old-fashioned bell

and the children at that school
didn't know everyone
who lived within ten kilometres
and then she stopped talking
and smiled . . .
at the end of the day
Ms Arthur told us
she was going to apply
to stay at our school
for another year
at least!

MICK

Why is it always Charlie Deakin
who's asked to lead me
to the Principal's office?
What have I done this time!
Charlie is smirking, again,
does he have any other look?
Why do I need him to show me
where Mr Hume's office is?
Charlie knocks on the door
and says, 'Mick Dowling's here, sir.'
As he walks away, he mutters, 'Again'
and I so much want to chase him,
but Mr Hume calls me inside
and tells me to sit down.
He stands at the window
gazing outside
and I'm tempted to just admit everything.
Yes, sir, I did it,
whatever it was. Guilty!
A week's detention?
Thanks, sir.
Like removing a bandaid from a scab,

just rip it off,
get it over and done with.
A second of pain
and then a numb feeling
for the rest of the day.
'Mick,' Mr Hume says.
I sit up a little straighter.
'Mick Dowling,' he repeats.
I know my own name.
'I believe you're responsible . . .'
here we go
'. . . for the biscuits
that were brought to school recently.'
Is he mad at me for not offering him one?
'Is that true, Mick?'
Well, strictly speaking, it was me
and Rachel, Cameron, Pete, Selina, Alex,
the whole gang
but I don't want them to get in trouble
so I say,
'Yes, sir, it was me.'
Mr Hume sits down
heavily at his desk
and clasps his hands in front of him.
'And I believe the biscuits

were given to the Kindy children,
and Year Five,
the teachers,
and Year Four,
in fact,
most of the school!'
I knew it! I knew it!
We should have given him one.
Diet or no diet.
Mr Hume sighs
and stands once again,
before walking to the window.
What is out there?
He says,
'A few people have mentioned
how pleased they were,
to see such sharing
in the schoolyard.
Such . . .'
Here we go, another lecture.
'. . . a sense of community.'
I groan, 'Sorry, sir.'
'I'm very proud of your actions, Mick!'
Did he say *proud*
not ashamed

not annoyed

not disappointed?

Mr Hume walks back to his desk

and offers his hand

for me to shake

and I stand quickly

and grip his hand firmly

like my dad taught me

and I say, 'Thanks, sir.'

'A very generous gesture, young man,' he says.

As I open the door to leave,

he says, once again, 'Well done, Mick'

and I turn and say,

'Next time, sir, I'll bring you a bundle as well.'

He grins,

'The diet, Mick . . .

Just the one, hey?'

PETE

Last night at dinner
Mum and Nan cooked a roast
with thin-sliced potatoes baked in the oven,
just the way I like them,
and pumpkin and broccoli from our garden
and Dad made his favourite pepper sauce
for pouring gloopily over the roast
and me and Dad
moved the kitchen table and chairs
out to the verandah
for the breeze
and Dad let me pour
him and Nan
a glass of beer each
but Mum touched her tummy
and said no
when I offered her a glass.
Maybe she's sick?
And I filled Ursula and my glasses
with sweet raspberry cordial.
We all sat outside
eating and drinking

and halfway through the meal
Dad clinked his glass with a spoon
and stood up,
'Nan, Pete, Ursula . . .
guess who's pregnant?'
Ursula giggled, 'You, Dad!'
and everyone laughed
but we all looked at Mum,
her face had gone as red
as the cordial in my glass
and, just for a second,
I saw Nan glance
across the paddock
to the cemetery
where Grandpa is buried
and then she reached over
and hugged Mum tightly.
Mum had gone from blushing
to crying
and she hugged Nan back
and said,
'If it's a boy,
I know what we'll name him.'
And Nan smiled.

LAURA

After school
I visit Mr Korsky,
with the last chocolate crackle.
He winks as he takes my gift, and says,
'Wait just a minute, young lady.'
He shuffles over to the back of his shed
and comes back with a small tin.
It's shiny and new and doesn't have a label.
Mr Korsky reaches for his screwdriver
and lifts the lid.
He offers it to me,
'Hold it up to your nose.'
Inside is a golden liquid,
like honey, only darker and thicker,
sweet and treacly and . . .
a smell so familiar.
Mr Korsky laughs,
'Someone . . . a kind young student
left me a batch of recipes.'
He nods at the tin I hold,
'Lavender molasses.
Perfect for scones or toast,

almost as tasty as this chocolate crackle!'
He places a cushion on a drum
and offers me a seat.
He says, quietly,
'If you know who left the recipes,
thank them for me, will you?'

CAMERON

On Saturday morning,
I nervously enter the newsagency,
expecting Mrs Davenport to yell
and point me to the door
as soon as I walk in
but
she just folds her arms across her chest
like Dad does when he's angry
and I swallow hard
walking quickly to the counter
and I place the cake tin in front of her
and she says,
'What's this?'
I'm too nervous to answer
so
she unfolds her arms
and opens the tin.
The smell of biscuits,
fresh-baked this morning,
fills the shop
and she leans down
over the tin

closes her eyes
and takes a deep breath.
I glance quickly towards the comics
and she catches me looking
only this time
she smiles
and says,
'Ten minutes',
reaching for a biscuit,
'and not a second more, you hear.'

MICK

On the other side of the school back fence
there is a paddock full of lush wild grass
and there are nanny goats and their kids
who wander around and bleat
and sleep sometimes in the thick grass
with just their ears poking up.
In the gully is the river
surrounded by willow trees
with their branches weeping low,
brushing along the surface.
And sometimes when the sun is high
and you look really close you can see
little silver fish darting around.
On the eastern bank of the river
someone has tied a rope to one of the trees
and if you're tall enough
you can grab the rope and swing yourself
far out above the water
and if you wanted
on a hot sunny day
if you're wearing swimmers,
and it's lunchtime

and no one saw you jump the back fence,
you could drop into the water and swim,
laughing all the way to the sandy shore
watched only by the goats
and the glorious sunshine.
When you were dry and dressed,
back in your school uniform
and sneaking across the paddock
hiding in the long grass,
before climbing the fence back to school
you'd notice
someone has written the word
paradise
on the river side of the fence
where no one can see it but you.
In the last few seconds before you return to school.

CAMERON'S DELICIOUS ANZAC BISCUITS

1 cup plain flour, sifted
1 cup rolled oats
1 cup shredded coconut
¾ cup brown sugar
125 grams butter, chopped
2 tablespoons golden syrup
½ teaspoon bicarbonate of soda
1 tablespoon water

Help your mum make this recipe! Preheat the oven to 160°C. Grease a baking tray with butter or line with non-stick baking paper.

Combine the plain flour, rolled oats, shredded coconut and brown sugar in a large bowl.

In a saucepan over low heat, melt the butter and golden syrup. Remove from heat. Dissolve the bicarbonate of soda in the water, and then stir into the golden syrup liquid.

Pour the liquid over the dry ingredients and mix until well combined.

Roll spoonfuls of the biscuit mixture into balls and place them on the baking tray, 4–5 centimetres apart. Flatten the balls slightly with a fork (or the palm of your hand!).

Bake biscuits in the oven for 20 minutes or until golden brown. Wait until the Anzac biscuits cool before eating (I didn't!).

LAURA'S CRISP AND SWEET CHOCOLATE CRACKLES

4 cups Rice Bubbles
1 cup icing sugar, sifted
1 cup desiccated coconut
5 tablespoons cocoa powder (Too much chocolate is never enough!)
250 grams Copha, chopped

In large bowl, mix together the Rice Bubbles, icing sugar, desiccated coconut and cocoa powder.

Melt Copha in the microwave on a low heat. Allow to cool slightly.

Stir the melted Copha into the Rice Bubbles mixture until all ingredients are well combined.

Spoon the mixture into patty cake papers and chill in the refrigerator until the crackles are set and ready to eat.

UNTANGLING SPAGHETTI
Steven Herrick

Are toenails a good source of vitamin c?

What are ten things you will never hear your parents say?

And, more importantly, how do you untangle spaghetti?

A collection of humorous, touching and thought-provoking poems celebrating the everyday lives of children through topics as wide-ranging as food, animals, school, friends and sport – especially soccer!

> 'You know a book is a big hit when your child keeps laughing out loud, then starts using phrases from it in everyday conversations. It's a bigger hit when parents join in. We give gigantic ticks to Herrick's book of poems.' *Herald Sun*

> 'Herrick's poetry is playful and insightful, funny and poignant . . . This new compilation is highly recommended.' *MAGPIES*

> 'The king of poetry for children is Steven Herrick. Herrick's poems – and, indeed, this collection on the whole – are so well balanced. On the one hand there's humour and light-heartedness; on the other there's depth and thoughtful care . . . this vivid poetry shows that good things can come in small packages.' *Sydney Morning Herald*

> 'It is a dangerous book, so be sure to bring it out when all of you are ready to be shocked, delighted, tickled and outraged.' *Reading Time*

ISBN 978 0 7022 3730 0

RHYMING BOY
Steven Herrick

father (fah'dh–) n. 1. Someone who is meant to live with you, answer your questions, NOT watch soaps and most importantly take you to father-son events.

Jayden Hayden, wordsmith, a.k.a rhyming boy, doesn't have a dad – just a mum obsessed with Jayden Finch, the footballer, and an embarrassing name that gets him teased. When a school father-son day is announced, Jayden's quest for answers becomes a puzzle he needs to solve, and quickly.

Could Jayden Finch be more than just a footballer? With the help of his an-answer-to-every-question friend Saskia, he aims to track down his namesake and his father all in one go.

From the award-winning poet and author Steven Herrick comes a novel about a young boy's search for family, friendship and well . . . footballers.

> 'The most gorgeous book I've read in a long time, *Rhyming Boy* starts with the brilliant chapter 'The street of silly names' and never lets up in any way. *Rhyming Boy* is packed with beautiful, fully-developed characters who make the reader laugh and cry. Herrick's use of words, rhythm and linguistic tricks makes this story absorbing on many levels. This is a special book that you should mark down as a "must read".' *Buzz Words*

> 'This is a fun read, full of gentle, teasing humour. It is a well paced, interesting and quite moving story with many funny and quirky characters.' *Reading Time*

> 'From page one, line one, word one, I was absorbed by Steven Herrick's *Rhyming Boy*.' *Australian Book Review*

ISBN 978 0 7022 3673 0

UQP